THE KEMP GAMBIT

NICKY PENTTILA

I

THE KEMP GAMBIT

THE SEISMIC MONITOR'S orange-green glow painted Dr. Brianna Aguilar's face sickly as she leaned forward, squinting at patterns that shouldn't exist. Outside Kemp Research Station, the Antarctic wind shrieked, rattling the corrugated walls and sending vibrations through the floor that she could feel in her bones. The coffee in her thermos had gone cold an hour ago, leaving a bitter film on her tongue, but she couldn't tear herself away from the screen.

Fourteen months. That's how long she'd been monitoring the mélange dynamics of the Kemp Ice Shelf—the jumbled pack of sea ice, snow, and shattered bergs that choked its natural rifts like mortar in a massive wall. Fourteen months of analyzing every tremor, every crack, every subtle shift in the thousands of gigatons of ice between Kemp station and the open ocean. She knew this ice shelf the way a pianist knows their favorite sonata. Every natural rhythm, every expected variation.

This wasn't natural.

The lab around her hummed with the constant background noise of Antarctic isolation: the wheeze of heat pumps working overtime against the minus-forty cold, the distant generator's diesel rumble that kept them all alive, the sharp crack-pop of ice expanding and contracting somewhere nearby. Hot plastic from re-soldered electronics on the scored-wood tech tables mixed with the perpetual hint of diesel fuel that permeated every-thing at Kemp Station. Her clothes, her hair, even the inside of her nose carried that sharp, industrial tang that marked life here at the bottom of the world.

Usually, she liked working the odd shift, when Richardson's CD player wasn't blaring and people weren't opening and slamming the door all the time. But now she wished somebody else was here, to look. To listen. To convince Brianna that she was wrong.

She bumped up the seismic array's sensitivity, her breath fogging the screen despite the lab's heat-ing. Confirmed: the data from the sensors posi-tioned across the ice shelf told a story that made her stomach clench. Compression waves with mathematical precision. Perfect timing intervals. Disturbances clustered around three specific coordinates—the underwater ridges that provided the ice shelf's structural backbone.

"Come on," she whispered, pulling up the timestamps. Six-hour intervals. Each disturbance had occurred during shift changes over the past three days, when personnel movement and equipment operations would mask any unusual surface activity.

It couldn't mean what she thought it meant.

The wind outside hit a new octave, and somewhere in the station's superstructure, metal groaned against the cold. Brianna had grown to love these sounds during her first Antarctic winter —the station's voice, proof of human engineering holding fast against the planet's most hostile environment. Tonight, they felt ominous.

She cross-referenced the seismic data with her mélange measurements, fingers flying across the keyboard despite the awkward bulk of her fleece gloves. The numbers that appeared made her breath catch in her throat.

Twelve meters. Last month: fifteen meters. Two months ago: seventeen meters.

The slush mixture filling the shelf's rifts was thinning faster than any of their climate models predicted. At ten meters, the critical threshold, rift propagation could begin. Below ten meters, the entire shelf could experience catastrophic failure—not the gradual calving that characterized normal ice shelf behavior, but a complete structural collapse that could happen in hours.

She pulled up satellite imagery from the past week, overlaying it with her seismic readings. The Kemp Ice Shelf stretched before her in false-color glory, a massive tongue of ice fed by the inland glacier, buttressed by those three crucial under-water ridges that showed up as dark shadows in the bathymetric data. Pinning points, glaciologists called them. Remove the pinning points, and eighteen trillion tons of ice became eighteen trillion tons of floating debris.

Someone pushed the heavy lab door behind Brianna open with a grunt. The metal door's thick seals creaked and groaned as it swung just enough for Sarah Kaiako to slip through. The marine biolo-gist carried the smell of the outdoors with her—that clean, sharp scent of air so cold it seemed to crystallize in her nostrils.

As she trundled to her computer setup, Sarah unwound her face mask, shaking ice crystals from her dark hair. Her cheeks were bright red with cold.

"Still up? It's the middle of the night." Sarah's favorite joke. They were only a month into the continent's one hundred five straight days of dark.

"Just trying to make sense of some readings." Brianna gestured at the screen. Another set of eyes could see whatever Brianna was missing. "Main seismic array's picking up some unusual patterns."

Sarah approached, squinting at the wavelength displays. She'd taken her outer coat off but her inner coat looked frigid stiff.

"Equipment malfunction? Been a bad day for that. I had to restart my aquarium pumps three times already." Must be what caused the blaring alarms coming from the other lab earlier.

"That's what I thought, at first. But it's been two days." Brianna pulled up a comparison chart, showing last month's ice movement patterns alongside the anomalous readings. "Look at the regularity. Natural ice dynamics are chaotic—thermal expansion, tidal stress, gravitational settling, all that. It should be a jumble, a fun puzzle. But these last few days, This looks almost…"

She trailed off, unable to voice the word that had been haunting her thoughts.

"Almost?" Sarah said.

"Engineered."

Sarah put her thick-gloved hand on the back of Brianna's office chair and leaned past her. They stared at the screen together, the lab's heating system cycling on with a mechanical wheeze. Outside, the wind's voice rose and fell like a tide of sound, carrying with it the vast presence of the Antarctic continent—millions of square kilometers of ice and stone that had been waiting here since before humans evolved, indifferent to their small warm bubble of artificial life.

"Is this bad?" Sarah finally said.

"Potentially."

Brianna winced. Tell the truth. "Catastrophic."

Sarah sucked in a breath. She was acting station leader, with Curtis out after an emergency appendectomy. After the surgery had been successful, Volkov had joked that Sarah, the emergency surgeon since she was a veterinarian, had missed her chance to take over the station. But Sarah was leader based on time in service, not because she wanted to be in charge.

"You're sure?" Sarah asked. "Did you check with anyone?"

Brianna went cold, and then hot. One mistake, one stupid mistranslated temperature, and nobody trusted her. Then again, this was bigger than one misaligned temp-scale reading. And she already had checked with someone.

"Sent yesterday's data to the team at Stanford," she said.

"And the Geo chat?"

"Was waiting to hear back." Was waiting for the brains at Stanford to tell her she was wrong.

Sarah harrumphed. "Who else has access to the remote seismic monitoring equipment?" she said.

Really, anyone on Kemp Station's twelve-person crew. Security was practically nil, with everybody too focused on surviving and, ideally, avoiding frostbite.

"Peter Volkov, of course." The station's surly field safety coordinator from Alabama, of all places. "The whole climate team could, but probably just Richardson. And Curtis and you."

Brianna didn't want to think of them as suspects.

But it sure was suspicious.

"Peter knows explosives," Sarah said, tapping the back of the chair—and Brianna's shoulder—in thought. "Ice management, controlled demolitions for emergency access routes. But I don't think he's been exploding anything lately." A deep whoop of wind outside made her shudder. "But who knows, in this noise."

Brianna shivered. She'd been avoiding that train of thought, but Sarah was right. Peter had both the technical knowledge and physical access required to generate the patterns she was seeing.

"I should ask him about it in the morning," Brianna said, trying to keep her voice casual. "The real morning. Maybe he's noticed something I missed."

Sarah nodded, but her expression remained troubled. "Brianna, if these readings are what they look like… if someone is deliberately destabilizing the ice shelf…"

"Bad news." Brianna's training took over, her voice becoming clinical as she explained the science that terrified her. "The Kemp Ice Shelf provides crucial buttressing for the inland glacier. Remove that support, and we're looking at accelerated ice flow that could contribute 1.5 meters to global sea level rise within five years. Coastal cities worldwide would be uninhabitable. The number of refugees, I don't know. A hundred million?"

The numbers hung in the air between them. Sarah wrapped her arms around herself. Brianna realized she was doing the same thing.

"Okay," Sarah whispered. "So ping Stanford again. And put the data on the chat. We can afford to look stupid. We can't afford to be wrong."

THE MESS HALL at 0800 hours buzzed with the familiar sounds of breakfast—the scrape of spoons against bowls, the hiss of the coffee machine working overtime, the low murmur of conversation that marked the beginning of another day at the bottom of the world.

The place was bustling. Everybody was up, all remaining eleven of them with poor Curtis still out sick. Most clumped at one of the two round plain-metal tables, with a few outliers at the two-tops against the wall. Brianna sat with her back to the wall, a habit she'd developed during fieldwork that now felt prescient.

The smell of reconstituted eggs and bacon couldn't quite mask the underlying diesel fume that pervaded everything at Kemp Station, but her stomach rumbled anyway. She'd managed maybe three hours of sleep, her dreams filled with collapsing ice and rising seas.

An hour ago, Wiggins at Stanford had confirmed her interpretation of the readings. Something was really wrong. It was not a curious penguin adopting one of the sensors again. Or rather, three curious penguins, at three distinct, very specific, very dangerous points.

Somebody here had done something. Unless some unplanned flight dropped a secret saboteur. Better story, but her sensors would have picked that up. And Peter Volkov's radar.

He sat two tables away, methodically working through his breakfast while reading something on a tablet. In the unflattering lighting, his face looked pale, drawn. The laugh lines that usually only crinkled around his eyes when he told wild stories about his previous Antarctic deployments seemed deeper, carved by something more than cold, dry air.

Brianna watched him covertly while pretending to focus on her oatmeal. Peter's thick hands, scarred from years of outside work, moved with their usual steady precision as he ate. Those hands had access to demolition equipment, to the shaped charges used for routine ice management around the station. Those hands could place explosives with the precision required to destabilize pinning points at specific coordinates.

Stop it. She was building a case against a colleague based on speculation and circumstantial evidence. But the seismic data, if true, didn't lie, and Peter was one of the few people at Kemp Station with both the knowledge and access required to create those artificial signatures.

James Richardson, the mission's senior climatologist, claimed the chair across from her with the weary sigh of someone who'd been fighting some distant bureaucracy all morning. His graying beard held ice crystals from his brief walk across the compound, and he carried with him the sharp tang of extreme cold. All the men had beards by now, though Richardson's still hadn't filled in.

"Equipment problems in the met station," he announced, grabbing the plastic pepper shaker and dousing his eggs. "Third temperature sensor failure this month. This place is absolute hell on electronics."

"I've been having issues with the seismic monitoring array," Brianna said, seizing the opening. "Getting some unusual readings that don't match known ice movement patterns."

Richardson looked up with interest. His expertise in Antarctic climate systems made him one of the few people at the station who could immediately understand the implications of her data. "What kind of unusual? Instrument malfunction or something more interesting?"

"That's what I'm trying to figure out." Brianna kept her voice casual, scientific. "The compression wave patterns are regular—mathematically regular. Too regular for natural ice dynamics. I was hoping to cross-reference with Peter's safety monitoring equipment, see if he's noticed anything anomalous."

She glanced toward Peter's table as she spoke. He was still reading his tablet, but something in his posture had changed—a subtle tension that suggested he was listening to their conversation despite his apparent focus on the screen.

Richardson followed her gaze. He leaned forward, toward Brianna.

"Volkov's been acting strangely lately," he said

quietly. "Spending a lot of time in the equipment bay, taking the Hägglunds out to the ice shelf at odd hours. When I asked him about it, he said he was updating emergency cache locations, but…"

"But?" Brianna prompted.

Richardson shrugged, the gesture constrained by his heavy fleece under-jacket. "Could be nothing. This isolation gets to everyone differently. But he's been checking his satellite phone constantly, like he's expecting important news."

Before Brianna could respond, Peter himself approached their table. He loomed over Richardson, blocking the light to the table. Up close, the changes in his appearance were more pronounced—dark circles under his eyes, a nervous energy in his movements that seemed at odds with his usual calm competence. He carried his coffee mug like a shield, both hands wrapped around its warmth.

"Morning, Richardson. Brianna." His voice carried its usual soft Southern accent, but underneath was a strain she'd never heard before. "I heard you go on about seismic monitoring. Anything I can help with?"

Brianna's heart stuttered. She nearly swallowed a breath. Stay calm.

"Odd readings over the past few days," she said, voice steady. "Compression wave patterns.

Wondering if your on-ground safety equipment has detected anything similar."

Peter's eyes flicked away from her face for just a moment—toward the tiny flat rectangle of a window that looked out over the ice shelf.

"Nope," he said. "Nothing special. Might just be your calibration's off. You know how the cold shocks everything."

A reasonable explanation, technically sound. But something in Peter's voice, the way he avoided direct eye contact, set off every alarm bell. Brianna had spent years learning to distinguish between natural phenomena and human interference in data sets.

Peter's response felt like interference—careful, calculated, designed to deflect rather than illuminate.

"Sure, but it worries me," she pressed. "Could be bad news." She tried to catch his gaze, failed.

"How bad?" Richardson cut in.

"Really bad."

Peter was suddenly backing away from their table, coffee mug at full shield. Brianna raised her voice, as if that would help make her point.

"If I could cross-reference our data, compare timestamps, you know, it would ease my mind."

"Sure, sure. I'll pull the data for you." He looked out the window again. "Later. This afternoon. Storm system's moving in tomorrow, want to make sure everything's tied down tight."

He hurried away, weaving between tables toward the far exit, toward the big garage and diesel storage.

Richardson leaned forward conspiratorially.

"That was interesting. Peter's usually eager to discuss technical problems—it's what he lives for. I've never seen him deflect questions like that."

Brianna frowned. "Neither have I."

THE MORNING PROGRESSED with the station's usual rhythms, except for Brianna. She was edgy, flighty, hyperaware of every sound, every movement: from her colleagues, from the building, from the grumbling wind outside. The grumbling wind that would hit gale force tomorrow, according to the forecasts.

She tried to focus on routine tasks—updating ice shelf mélange shifts, calibrating sensors, reviewing climate data—but her attention kept drifting to the seismic monitoring array and the increasingly damning pattern of artificial disturbances. She'd started running simulations, trying to predict the effects of destabilization. None were good, and some were downright terrifying.

By noon, she'd decided. She had to go get a look at those sensors. Whatever was making that noise, they had to get rid of it.

She tucked a couple protein bars and a jug of warm water in her outer jacket, stomped into her double-lined boots, wrapped her head and hands, and headed out.

Even through her cold-pinched nose, the equipment bay, just inside the big truck garage, smelled of machine oil and diesel. Brianna gathered what she needed for a solo reconnaissance trip: more extreme weather clothing, emergency communication equipment, portable seismic sensors. One of the Hägglunds tracked vehicles sat close in the adjacent garage, its orange paint bright against the gray concrete. Peter must have taken the other one.

She'd driven similar vehicles during previous Antarctic missions. Built for ice shelf travel, they were amphibious and virtually unstoppable in polar conditions. But she hadn't needed to travel in one this mission.

She'd checked the spare wheels and was checking the vehicle's fuel tanks when a voice behind her made her freeze.

"Going somewhere?"

Peter stood in the doorway between the equipment room and the garage, silhouetted against the brighter inner room's lighting. His orange jacket and Spartan green knit cap made him look like a skinny pumpkin, and his voice carried no threat. But there was something in his posture that made Brianna's hand move unconsciously toward the emergency radio clipped to her belt.

"Need eyes on those sensors," she said, trying to project calm confidence. "Home Base thinks the readings are ice buildup or some mechanism winding down."

Peter stepped into the bay, and she could see his face clearly now. The strain she'd noticed at breakfast had intensified, carving deep lines around his mouth. His face looked gray against the black of his beard. He looked like a man carrying an impossible burden.

And a harpoon gun.

"I'll drive," he said.

Brianna's breath stopped. The gentle cloud of exhale around her dissipated as she stared at Peter Volkov. She needed to see those sensors. But if he was the one who did whatever had been done, if something had been done, he surely wouldn't let her see it. Or report back.

She could not say yes.

She could not say no. Two was better than one; standard safety procedure. He was the outside security expert, an outdoors cat. She was a soft little researcher, definitely an indoors cat.

Shit.

He didn't even wait for her answer, just turned back into the equipment room to load up on gear. He was faster than her, stronger, smarter about the terrain. And he had that gun.

But she'd have it, inside. The tie-down for the harpoon gun was on the passenger side. She didn't exactly know how to use it; but she knew how to keep him away from it, as least.

That left knives, crowbar, his plain old hands, and—oh yes—getting kicked out of the vehicle and freezing to death.

But not alone.

Brianna ran to the equipment room just as Peter exited it. She picked up three more batteries for her satellite phone, and two more for the tablet, and jammed them into her black tools backpack. She'd just leave the audio on the thing on, if she had to. The phone would send; the tablet would record. On the way around to the passenger side of the Hägglunds, the cloud of exhale around her was thick.

The tracked vehicle's engine turned over with a deep rumble that filled the bay. Blessedly warm air began flowing from its heating vents within moments.

Brianna had to climb into the passenger seat. The Hägglunds was built like a small gray-metal living room that happened to have tracks instead of wheels. The cabin was spacious enough for four people, with padded bench seats covered in heavy-duty vinyl that had been scarred by years of Antarctic service. Every surface was designed for functionality—grab rails bolted to the roof, storage compartments built into the walls, emergency equipment secured in brackets that looked like they could survive a rollover. She slid her phone under the netting tacked onto the high ridge between driver and front passenger, screen off, microphone on.

The dashboard belonged on a piece of construction equipment rather than a passenger vehicle, dominated by gauges for engine temperature, hydraulic pressure, and track tension. A military-style radio mounted above the windshield crackled with static, while a GPS unit showed their position as a single green dot surrounded by vast expanses of black. Synthetic seat materials, diesel fumes from the heating system, and the scent of hydraulic fluid mixed with the lingering smell of wet wool.

Peter settled easily into the driver's seat. He didn't look at her, just danced his thick-gloved fingers across controls that looked like a spaceship's. Switches for differential locks, buttons for track tensioning, levers that controlled the vehicle's amphibious capabilities. The Hägglunds could traverse ice, snow, water, and marsh with equal confidence, perfect for the Antarctic, where solid ground could change to liquid surface without warning.

Out of the garage, they were soon off the short main track and onto the sastrugi, the sharp wave-like snow and ice formations of the polar fields. Brianna was glad for the big noise-canceling head-phone-earmuff things. The roar of the engine was bad enough, but the clatter of the rubber tracks slapping over ice and snow was deafening.

The world outside was shades of blue-gray and white, the horizon a wide vague line between the dark sky and the shadowed snow. Nautical twilight, when the only sunlight that reached them was what bounced down from the upper atmosphere. No aurora, but the moon was out today, which was good for satellite communication, not because it was the moon but because a lot of satellites liked to follow its orbit.

Inside the Hägglunds, through its small wind-shield and side windows, the ice and snow looked otherworldly, atmospheric, soft.

Deadly.

"I've never actually driven one of these, in the cold," Brianna admitted over their shared audio line. She ran her hand along the only slightly simpler part of the dashboard that faced her. The heating system was already making the cabin comfortable, transforming the space into a warm bubble isolated from the hostile environment outside.

"They're incredible machines," Peter said, his voice oddly hollow. "Swedish engineering. Can go anywhere, survive anything. I've taken this one across crevasse fields, through whiteout conditions, over ice that was barely thick enough to support our weight." He hit the first swoop of ice hard. "Completely reliable. Unlike people."

Okay.

"Give me your sat phone," Peter said. He moved his left hand to twelve o'clock on the steering wheel and held his right hand out.

Brianna shrunk away from his hand. Suddenly she was too hot. The harpoon, in front of her over the window, was netted in. She'd need a minute to get it out. He could do so much to her in a minute.

"Why?"

"Match it up to Aggie, here." He waved his hand at the sat phone in the cradle on the dashboard between them.

"Aggie?"

"Nickname."

"For Texas A & M? I thought their color's maroon."

"Not on a certain January one, Year of Our Lord

two thousand and five. When Tennessee painted them Volunteer bright up and down that Cotton Bowl field." He didn't smile, exactly, but he sounded satisfied. "My last game."

Brianna's shoulders eased. She pulled her satellite phone out of the backpack and set it in Peter's hand.

He held it up so he could read the screen and still drive.

And powered it down.

He tucked the now-dead phone into the netting attached to his door.

"Let's talk," he said.

Shit.

Brianna pasted her gaze out the front window of the Hägglunds. At the wind-swirled snow a couple miles away, at the blue-black ragged mountains way off. Anywhere but at the tablet on the hump between her seat and Peter's. It was still recording audio. Even in the din of the cracking ice under the vehicle's treads and the blowing of the heater and the growling of the wind, it would filter and catch their words.

She hoped.

Twenty minutes to the first sensor location, according to the GPS on the dashboard. Twenty minutes to the next. Thirty minutes to the last one. Sixty minutes home.

No one said anything for three loud minutes. Four. Five.

"Okay," Brianna said.

"Suppose something happened to the ice shelf —it got split up somehow. Would that be so bad?"

It would be catastrophic. Bigger than catastrophic. Apocalyptic.

"Peter," she said, careful, "why are you asking me that?"

He wouldn't look at her.

"Here's a story. My daughter Emma is eight years old," Peter said, his voice barely audible even with the ear muffs. "She has this rare genetic condition—mitochondrial myopathy. Born with it. Her muscles don't process energy correctly. She's been in a wheelchair since she was five, and it's getting worse. It will always get worse."

Not always.

Brianna's throat tightened. Kids, didn't they just rip your heart out. "Peter…"

"There's an experimental treatment. Gene therapy that could halt the progression, maybe even reverse some of the damage. But it's not approved by insurance, costs six hundred thousand dollars just to start, and even then there's a waiting list."

He checked the GPS and then turned thirty degrees to the left. It didn't look like the field was any easier riding this way. "My wife Elena lost her job six months ago. Downsized. We've already mortgaged everything, sold everything we could. We're three months behind on medical bills and six months behind on our house payments."

He paused. His sigh made her ears ring. He couldn't be saying what he was saying.

"Someone contacted you," she said.

Peter nodded. "Online support forum for security folks, us who work alone a lot. I'd been venting, about money, about the cold and the wind, about feeling trapped down here while my family fell apart back home, you know. The usual stuff—that's what the place is for."

Brianna wondered why there wasn't a parallel support forum for researchers. They got cold and had money and family problems, too.

Peter hit the defog on the windows. "This person—they called themselves 'Arctic Solutions'—they seemed to know everything about me. About Emma's condition, about our financial problems, even about the specific capabilities of Kemp Station."

"What did they want you to do?"

"They said they needed someone with technical access who could cause a minor safety incident that would force early station closure. Make it look like equipment failure or environmental hazard.

Everyone would be evacuated ahead of schedule, the insurance would cover the financial losses, and I'd get eight hundred thousand dollars." Peter's voice grew increasingly strained. "Made it sound like insurance fraud, not sabotage. Like I'd be helping everyone go home early while getting enough money to give to the hospital to make Emma whole."

Brianna frowned. Shitty insurance scammers, sounded like.

Until you looked at the facts.

"You set charges," she said. "Timed, so they would go off when you were nowhere near." That was the regularity she was seeing: itty-bitty ticking clocks.

The bombs were locked and loaded.

And in precisely the right spots.

"They gave you the coordinates." She didn't even say it as a question.

"Said they were structural weak points where small charges would create visible damage without catastrophic failure. They had technical diagrams, stress analysis reports, engineering data. It all looked completely legitimate."

To a security specialist.

"They're at what we call the pinning points," Brianna said.

Peter looked at her sharply. "They have a name?"

"Peter, those aren't weak points for controlled damage. They're the underwater ridges that provide structural support for the entire ice shelf. Destroying one of them would cause major damage. All three, and you'll trigger complete collapse."

The color drained from Peter's face. The Hägglunds stopped; he must have taken his foot off the gas. "Complete collapse? But they said…"

"The Shelf would break in a matter of hours," she said. "In months, it would flood out millions of people. In five years, a hundred million—more— would be climate refugees."

The heating system's gentle hum seemed obscenely normal against the magnitude of what they were discussing. Peter stared through the windshield as if seeing the future that his desperation had potentially created—cities underwater, populations displaced, civilization reorganizing around a fundamentally altered coastline.

"Oh God," he whispered. He rested his head against the back of the seat and closed his eyes. His eyelids looked bruised.

"So you set charges?" Brianna asked. "When are they set to go off?"

She held her breath.

"Three hours, and some." Peter didn't open his eyes. "They're synchronized, one then the next then the next, at non-mathematical intervals. And I can't stop them—the detonation sequence is already locked in."

Three hours.

Impossible.

Impossible not to try.

"I was supposed to keep everyone on-base." Peter rubbed his rough glove against his eyes. His sigh filled the whole cabin. "Nobody would be to blame."

Well, they were out here now. In this wild, frigid blue-gray world that didn't know what was coming for it.

Brianna's mind lit up.

"How many charges? What type?"

"Six. Two shaped charges at each spot." Peter leaned forward, almost eager to talk tech specs. "PETN-based, designed for precision ice penetration."

"And you placed them exactly according to their specifications?" She knew he'd done it perfectly already, based on her readings.

"Every detail. I used diving equipment to position them at the precise coordinates, at the exact depths they specified." Peter's professional pride warred visibly with his growing horror. "I followed their instructions perfectly."

The irony was almost unbearable. Peter's technical competence, the same skills that made him valuable as a safety coordinator, had been weaponized against the very people he was supposed to protect. Sarah Kaiako and Dr. Richardson and poor Dr. Curtis and the eight other people who had trusted their lives to Peter's expertise.

And the tens of millions of others who thought their world was safe.

She needed to call someone. Get help.

More bitter irony: no help was coming. All the world had within three hours of these charges was her, an academic research scientist, and him, the man who executed the sabotage.

But maybe there was something there…

"There's something else," Peter continued. "The people who contacted me—they've been monitoring station communications. They know about your readings, about your investigation."

A chill that had nothing to do with Antarctic cold ran down Brianna's spine. A freezing-cold target on her back. "You're sure?"

"They sent me a message this morning. Said to keep you from going deeper, that it was important that you not discover the charges before detonation. After, nothing would be conclusive."

So that's why all her email was delayed. What messages had she never received?

"Even so." Peter looked directly at her for the first time since entering the vehicle. "Brianna, I'm starting to think they're planning to eliminate witnesses."

She couldn't even entertain that thought. Her mind glanced away from it and back to the bitter irony she'd been contemplating before.

"Are they listening to us now?"

"No, we're too far from the main dish for direct comms." He pulled out his phone, turned it off. "Just in case. And Aggie's Iridium handset phone is a direct link to base." A line-of-sight satellite call, not on the compromised station network.

Brianna pulled her laptop out of its warming case in her backpack. Still, it would have precious little battery life out here. She pulled up the sonar and sensor data on the screen, patched it over the land readings. Nothing had changed.

Everything had changed.

"If we can get to the charges in time, could you turn them off?"

"They'd know."

Shoot. She felt the ache of her back molars grinding, and made herself stop.

Wait.

"The same principles that make those charges dangerous—what if we turned it to our advantage," Brianna said, working the problem out loud as her fingers moved potential lines of force on the grid. "Instead of catastrophic failure, we could limit the damage. Manage the collapse, like they do with avalanches. Maybe even hold it off. Create fracture patterns that follow natural stress lines, directing the force into smaller, safer sections."

"Show me." Peter focused on the screen as if his eyes would burn holes in it. "Can we stop it?"

"Think so. If we can get at least three of these charges out of the water—maybe even two—and fiddle with the rest, I think we can do it."

"Cuts it close."

"It's not perfect," Brianna admitted. "We'd still get ice shelf failure, still get some acceleration of ice flow from the inland glacier. But instead of complete catastrophic collapse contributing 1.5 meters to sea level rise, we might limit it to 20-30 centimeters over several years."

"Manageable damage instead of global catastrophe?"

"Possible."

"Then what are we waiting for?" Peter hit the gas. The Hägglunds roar-crack-screeched into motion.

Brianna had to grab the nearest handrail to keep herself on the seat and her laptop in her lap.

To their west, the sky was swirling gray-blue-black. The beginning of the storm.

———

AT THE FIRST LOCATION, Brianna found herself appalled at the waste.

And grateful.

At the slight depression in the ice shelf surface that marked the location of the underwater ridge, Peter must have set up a thermal lance tripod, to open a hole to lower the charges into the water. You could only stay in the water five minutes, maybe ten, so it was smart to have the bomb as close to the right spot as possible before you got there.

Luckily for them, he'd been lazy, or wanted to get caught, or knew it didn't matter. He hadn't sealed the hole, and he hadn't bothered to dig up the industrial crampons he'd locked the lance to the ice with.

So they knew exactly where to put the winch.

He stopped the Hägglunds about fifty meters from the site, in the right spot to offer a windbreak while keeping safe distance from potential ice instability. The two of them would not be keeping a safe distance. The moment he switched off the engine, they heard the full voice of the Antarctic wind—a squealing roar that seemed to penetrate even the vehicle's insulated cabin.

"HOW, exactly, are we going to do this?" Brianna said.

"Winch first, then you go down and scoop up the charges." Peter handed her what looked like a golden ice pick. "Special tip fits into the two screws I set it in with."

"Me?"

He swiveled his seat and went to the back of the vehicle. Cupboards above and below the bench seats held diving gear sized small to extra large. He opened the far cupboard, pulled out what must be the smallest size, and shook it out.

"This is the shallowest site. You do this one, and then I can manage the other two."

"I go down, pull up the charges, and then what? Can you disarm them?"

Peter looked up from checking the diving tanks. "Affirmative." Then he left.

Brianna struggled into the diving gear with movements made clumsy by both the bulky equipment and her growing nerves. Outside was one thing, but outside and underwater?

The drysuit felt like wearing a personal submarine—thick neoprene and sealed seams that would keep her alive in water cold enough to stop her heart, but also restricted her mobility to the point where every movement required conscious effort.

Peter was back before she was ready. "Winch is ready."

"Remember," he said, helping her check equipment connections, "you'll have maybe five minutes of useful work time before the cold starts affecting your judgment and motor functions. The water is clear, but visibility will be limited by equipment lighting. Don't dawdle."

Outside the Hägglunds, the Antarctic wind hit her like a mallet made of ice. Even with full protective gear, the cold found ways to penetrate her defenses—around the edges of face masks, through microscopic gaps in equipment, into her lungs with every breath. The sound was overwhelming, a constant roar that made communication difficult even with radio equipment.

The winch didn't seem fazed by the atmospheric mallet. She'd drop down beside it and follow it to the hook at the end. The charges should be right there. Grab them, tug on the line, and let Peter pull her up.

Easy peasy.

She didn't feel the cold of the water; it felt the same as the air. But the water pressure—like ringing a bell with her the clapper inside. She let her hand curl around the winch line, let herself simply fall.

No seals, no penguins, not even fish. Did the animals feel the storm coming, too? She shivered, and instantly regretted it. Now she was even more aware of the cold.

There, the hook, and there, the bread-loaf-sized packets, parallel, gray against the blue-white of the ice. Brianna kept her hand on the line while she used the little pick to tap the new-formed ice off the screws holding metal band holding the bombs. When she had to let go, to actually unscrew them, her breaths started to double.

Bad news. Hyperventilation was never good. She spent a few precious brain computing time trying to calm herself down while also not dropping further. First screw came out easily, as did the second. But the metal band popped off.

The packet started to drop, into the darker depths of the water.

She could not let it drop. Even on the bottom of the shelf it would spread serious damage. Maybe critical.

Brianna grabbed at it, pivoting her body downward for maximum reach. Her hand with the pick was just long enough—she snagged it by the corner. As she pulled it toward her, she prayed that there was nothing in the corner—like the timing mechanism—that had been damaged.

No explosion, so that was good.

She tied it with a bungee to her thigh and pivoted back up to swim back to the second one. This time, she loosened only one screw, and held the package as she pulled it from its guard. Together with the first, they weighed as much as her work laptop.

She tugged on the cord, and let the line pull her up.

They packed the equipment back into the Hägglunds with all speed. No time to waste, and the weather was getting worse. Inside, out of the suit and back in her clothes, heat packs in all the pockets and in her boots and a mug of instant hot soup in her hands, Brianna watched Peter dismantle the bomb. Snap the detonator leads free of the booster, strip the timer's battery connector, separate the cap from the main charge. Just like he'd taught them in Kemp's safety briefing.

"Done," he said. "Easier than I thought."

He laughed at her expression.

THE SECOND PINNING point spot was eight kilometers from the first, but it took more than fifty minutes to get there. The minutes ticking away and the bone cracking bouncing of the Hägglunds was unendurable.

But they had to be this careful. They traveled across ice that showed increasing signs of stress from the approaching weather system. Crevasses that had been marked stable during previous traverses now showed widening gaps, and the vehicle's seismic sensors registered constant minor tremors as the ice shelf responded to wind pressure and temperature fluctuations.

At this rate, they weren't going to make it to the third one. Farthest away and, of course, at the most fragile section of the shelf.

The Hägglunds crested a pressure ridge, and suddenly they could see their destination through the blowing snow—another slight depression in the ice surface.

Aggie's sat-phone squawked.

"Brianna, are you there?" Sarah's voice was loud and clear.

Peter picked the phone up out of its holder. He handed the boxy thing to Brianna.

"Sarah?"

"Girl, what the heck are you doing? Storm's coming up, can't you see?"

"Just finishing up," Brianna lied.

"We see you on the map, way off to the south."

A pause. "Yes. Where that anomaly is. Check it later, Bree. Get home, now."

"On my way." Two lies in one conversation. Must be a new record for her.

She handed the phone back to Peter.

"You ready?"

This time, with the roles reversed—Peter in the water, Brianna on the winch—things went a lot faster. Well, one minute faster.

But afterward, getting the winch disconnected from the clamps and keeping a hold on it on the short trek back to the rover, was a bear. The wind gusted and scooped and slapped ice in their faces.

Packing it into the Hägglunds and throwing themselves back inside took nearly all the rest of Brianna's strength, and it looked like Peter's, too. He needed help getting the drysuit off, and needed hot soup to warm his fingers enough to manipulate the two new deadly packages.

"Thanks for telling me about the popping package, he said, his attention sunk into the second of the bomb mechanisms. "What time is it?"

Brianna was afraid to look. The farthest set of bombs was the first scheduled to detonate. Of course.

She forced herself to open the laptop. Look at the time.

"Three ten."

Less than an hour, and it would take most of an hour to get there.

"Should've gone there first," she said.

Peter ripped the timer mechanism away from the packet of fuel and set it carefully into one of his sodden dive boots.

"Mebbe." He shrugged. "Would have got us closer to home at the end."

The sat-com up in the front started squawking again. Sarah, more desperate.

"What's going on, Bree? Home base is freaked, and it can't be just the storm."

Brianna looked at Peter, his skin even paler and darker-splotched now that he'd been in and out of the water. His eyes, bloodshot, weary, determined.

Like her.

Peter turned the Hägglunds toward the last set of coordinates as Brianna stowed the last of the loose cargo.

Nobody answered Sarah.

TWENTY MINUTES LATER, the snow started swirling around them like a handsy old man. Forty minutes, and the wind stopped moaning and groaning and started shrieking in its version of fierce joy. Forty-five minutes later, and they were cresting the last ridge, seeing the familiar darker blue dip in the ice.

Detonation in ten minutes.

No time to set up the winch, even if Brianna could fight the wind to winch it. No time for either of them to get a cold and soggy drysuit on.

"Options," Brianna said.

"Thermal lance," Peter said. But he shook his head. He'd swapped his green knit cap for an orange one. "Blow it at the wrong time, but it still blows."

He tapped the driving wheel. "These are easy to move. Not screwed in. Just tucked into a crack in the shelf. Thought I'd be able to do it with all of them; had to come out a second time to finish the other two."

No wonder he left the crampons there.

"What about drop dive?" Brianna asked. Just go down, no line of safety, no visibility beyond your hand. These packets were set at the shallowest level, counterintuitive but damn effective, according to Brianna's and computer's calculations. "Might be a fast enough, if we put balloons on the packets to float them up faster than the diver." Because yeah, no chance the diver would make it back.

"You're not doing that," Peter said. He sighed. "And god help me, neither am I."

Sarah hadn't given up on them.

"God, Bree, I just heard from Stanford. They worried when you didn't respond. The ice shelf is breaking up? Get back here right now."

Brianna banged her head against the back of her seat. She wasn't going back, not like this. Going back to what? The base wasn't going to stand much longer, at this rate.

There had to be something else.

She banged her fist on the armrest. Looked out at the monster storm that was laughing, just laughing at them. Looked up.

There it was.

She turned to look at Peter, who was staring at the sat-phone.

"How good a shot are you, really?" she said.

Outside the Hägglunds, the Antarctic had grown genuinely murderous. Snow wasn't falling so much as being driven horizontally by wind that could strip exposed flesh in seconds. Even with her face double-wrapped, Brianna felt the cold like needles of ice along the sides of her face.

Even breathing became a conscious effort as the air temperature tried to freeze moisture in their lungs.

Each of them had a harpoon gun. Brianna's was the one-shot from the front cabin; Peter's a three-shot from storage. Four shots, and maybe one more if she could pull her harpoon's line back fast enough.

Four shots to save the world.

EVEN WITH THEIR earmuffs tucked into their face masks, the wind was a constant roar punctuated by freight-train gusts that threatened to lift them off their feet.

Brianna could feel her body temperature dropping despite multiple layers of insulation. Her fingers were becoming numb inside heated gloves, her thoughts slowing from the metabolic effects of extreme cold exposure. And here they were, operating complex equipment that required perfect precision.

Peter said the shot would be easier if they took it on their bellies, so they wrestled one of the space blankets onto the ground underneath them. He dropped a flare into the narrow hole in the ice that still remained from when he'd set these charges last week. They watched it slowly sink. The charges were down about as deep as Brianna was tall.

This was going to be hard.

She lined up her shot, slicing the clear black water with the red of her laser sight, aiming for the package on the right. Peter had said the chances she'd hit the mechanism and trigger the blow were slim to none. She took cold comfort in that. To endanger whole countries' worth of people this way—who would do such a thing? If this really was insurance fraud, it was global scale. Playing the markets. Capitalism at its finest.

It wasn't fraud. It was genocide.

Brianna pressed the trigger. The rebound hit her shoulder, hard. The line whirred as it paid out.

The harpoon hit nothing.

She shook her head no at Peter, tucked the gun under her knees, and started to pull her harpoon back up. The line was slick with ice the second it came out of the water.

Peter grabbed at her knee, pushed at her gun. Confused, she picked it up again. He held his gun —really a rifle—as if he were about to shoot, but looked at her instead. So she copied him, even pointing it down at the water, even though it wasn't loaded

But the tracking laser was still on. She could light the target to better help him aim.

She tried to hold still, against the wind, against the need for her body to shiver itself warm again. Kept the target lit.

Peter's first shot bagged the left-side packet.

He reeled it in quickly, set it between them, and settled down for shot two.

Which hit, but not the packet. It wedged itself maybe a hand's span above and to the right.

Peter really was a great shot.

He turned to her, waved at the packet between them, and shouted something. She shook her head. He tapped the top of his wrist. What time is it?

She pushed back the outer cuff of her jacket, and the inner. The wind grabbed the narrow band of skin, slashed at it as if to cut her hand off. The glass on her dad's hard-weather watch cracked, freezing the old-fashioned watch hands.

Four ten.

She tucked her thumb in and showed her hand to Peter. Four minutes left.

He waved at her to point her gun's light at the package again.

Brianna started to count. Three Mississippi for her to find the package in the dark water. Four Mississippi before the harpoon shot out.

And hit its target.

Brianna was up and turning for the Hägglunds when she thought she heard a shout. She turned back.

Peter was on his knees, leaning back, pulling hard against the reel of the gun, which was also pulling hard.

The line wasn't budging.

Brianna pointed her gun toward the water, swept the light from side to side.

The line of the harpoon that had gone wide had fouled the line that held the packet. The packet was just dangling on its line. Peter's tugging was fouling it more. If he could pull the first harpoon out, maybe they had a chance.

But it was an impossible angle. And empty harpoon guns.

Brianna held herself against a gust of wind—two Mississippis. Once she got her motion back, she waved a hand in front of Peter. She pointed to the water.

He saw the problem immediately, and must have seen that it was impossible, at least in the next ninety seconds. He threw down the gun and pulled out a giant hunting knife. He slammed the knife into the line, severing it.

The packet would fall to the bottom.

And then go off.

Brianna turned, and started to run.

Twenty-one Mississippis left.

They left the guns, the blanket, everything behind. As soon as she got into the Hägglunds Brianna grabbed the wire cutters, ready to hold out for Peter.

His door opened, and the wind seemed to slam him into the seat. He shook his right gloves off, started the vehicle, and reached out to her for his tools. The bomb rested on his left inner forearm like a baby.

He sliced into the wrapping for the fuel in his haste, but got the timer clear. Five Mississippis.

Peter took a deep breath, stilled his shaking hand, and did the thing.

Snap, strip, separate.

They'd done it.

He turned and looked at Brianna. For a moment, they smiled at each other, through the snow masks, the scarves, the droopy hoods of the jackets.

Then Hägglund bucked.

They'd almost done it.

"Brianna!" the sat-com screamed. "Get out of there! Giant ice slide, right under you."

Peter jammed the Hägglunds in reverse and backtracked a good soccer field's distance away from the ice hole before he pivoted it to face east.

"Home?" he said.

"Now," she said.

CHRISTCHURCH INTERNATIONAL SMELLED like floor polish and coffee. Brianna wrapped both hands around a paper cup hot enough to sting and watched the TV over the bar. The chyron crawled: Partial Failure at Kemp Ice Shelf; No One Hurt.

The feed cut to a live shot outside Scott Base: Sarah Kaiako in an orange parka, breath fogging, fielding questions. "A hero twice over," the anchor said—first for the emergency appendectomy, then for getting everyone off the base before the new Kemp Crevasse opened beneath the station.

Brianna was on her way to MIT, via Stanford and, perhaps, the Pentagon. The fractures had followed one of the sixteen pathways she'd modeled—no catastrophic break, but a managed failure. Significant, but manageable. Cities would have time to adapt.

"Mind if I sit?" Peter Volkov materialized with his own coffee. He looked ten years older and, somehow, lighter. A man in a navy windbreaker with a lanyard sat two tables back pretending to read the sports page.

Brianna tipped her cup. "How's your morning?"

He held up his phone: a text thread from an Assistant U.S. Attorney—see you Thursday; proffer session confirmed. "Cooperation agreement's signed. I'm a witness now. Sentencing will wait until after I testify." He flicked a glance at the windbreaker. "No one's calling it a walk."

"And little Emma?"

"Relocated for now. Elena's here, too. Witness-protection eval this afternoon." He tried a smile. "Emma thinks New Zealand accents are 'pirate-adjacent.'"

On the TV, the anchor switched to a split screen with a finance reporter. "Breaking: The FCA and the Monetary Authority of Singapore froze accounts linked to a 'climate risk strategies' unit at Orpheum Capital. Sources say the desk placed multi-billion-dollar positions that would have profited from rapid sea-level shocks."

Peter set his cup down. "There it is. They're gonna call it a rogue desk, God love 'em. DOJ unsealed two indictments in New York this morning. Interpol red notices for two principals. The rest got lawyered up."

"You gave them the messages?"

"Everything. The bonuses they wired me are sitting in an escrow account with the Marshals. Elena gets none of it." He rubbed his palms on his jeans. "I still planted the charges."

"You also helped take them out," Brianna said. "That matters."

He let that sit. "How's your inbox?"

"Ferocious. MIT wants me in a room with their climate engineering group." She nodded at the TV.

"And I get to help draft a paper that will be ninety percent redactions."

The anchor's tone softened. "Scientists tell us the partial failure will unfold over years. Coastal cities will have time to adapt."

Brianna watched a time-lapse of sea ice breathing in and out with the tide. "I'll take 'time' as a headline."

The PA crackled: "Air New Zealand flight to Boston via Auckland now boarding Group One."

She stood, shouldered her too-heavy bag again. The man in the windbreaker didn't look up, but he moved when Peter did.

"I should go talk to people who want to turn what we did out there into math," Brianna said. "You… keep breathing."

He rose, grimaced with a humorless kind of pride. "My lawyer says 'keep breathing' is excellent legal advice."

They walked together to the split in corridors where international departures branched. He stopped there. For a second the roar of the Antarctic felt like it had followed them, a phantom in the HVAC.

"Hey, Brianna."

She turned.

"Four shots to save the world," he said.

They bumped fists and peeled off in different directions.

48

ALSO BY NICKY PENTTILA

Cosmic Weave

Cooperative Realm: Frankie's Journeys

Cargo Trouble

Frankie Takes a Holiday

Frankie Takes a Dive

Frankie Finds a Dot

Frankie Takes a Bow

Cargo & Chaos: Frankie books 1 & 2

Cooperative Realm: The Arkhide Chronicles

Hidden Planet

The Listeners

The Elders of Arkhide

Tales of Arkhide story collection

Short Stories

Here: Earthbound Fantasies and Futures

There: Journeys to Imagined Realms

ABOUT THE AUTHOR

Nicky Penttila wrote her first story, a Mayan murder mystery, in seventh grade. But then came gymnastics, math team, and boyfriends. Later came husband, car payments, and a sleep-depriving work schedule at newspapers across the country. Then came a second career as a science writer. But the fiction kept trickling out, a story here, a novella there, and finally, a real live novel. And she hasn't stopped.

Find more great reads at nickypenttila.com